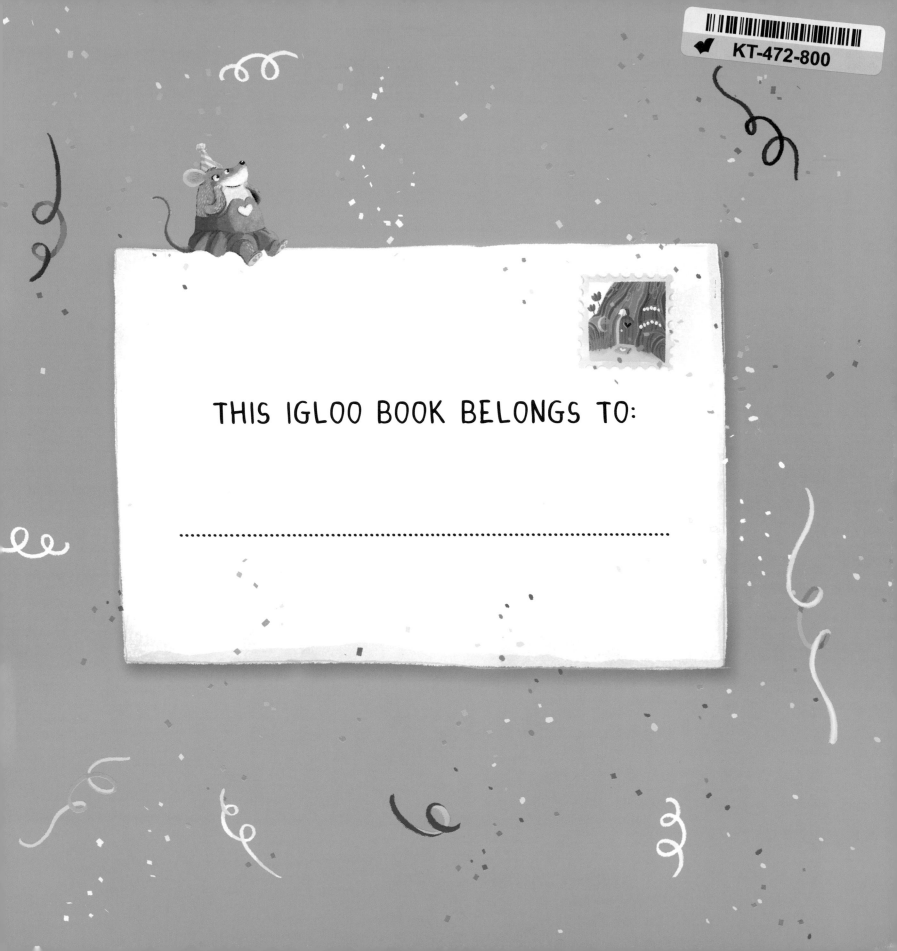

THIS IGLOO BOOK BELONGS TO:

....

igloobooks

Published in 2020
First published in the UK by Igloo Books Ltd
An imprint of Igloo Books Ltd
Cottage Farm, NN6 0BJ, UK
Owned by Bonnier Books
Sveavägen 56, Stockholm, Sweden
www.igloobooks.com

1120 002
2 4 6 8 10 9 7 5 3
ISBN 978-1-78670-873-1

Written by Stephanie Moss
Illustrated by Claudia Ranucci

Designed by Hannah George
Edited by Hannah Campling

Printed and manufactured in China

The BEST PARTY in the WORLD

igloobooks

Little Mouse was lonely and spent most days on her own
She had a quiet life in her mouse hole, all alone.

Best Friends

One day, she wrote an invitation and inside it said,

"Come to my tea party tomorrow. See you soon!" she read.

She addressed it to her mouse friend
to send the letter on its way.

Then she gave it to the Post Mouse
on his first stop of the day.

Before he delivered it, he stopped for a bite of cheese.

Then it flew...

Petal Cottage
2 Acorn Lane
Bluebell Wood
BFF M1CE

whoosh

... out of his bag on a sudden gust of breeze.

It flew **UP, UP** on the wind...

... into the farmyard
right next door.

Petal Cottage
2 Acorn Lane
Bluebell Wood
BFF M1CE

Petal Cottage
2 Acorn Lane
Bluebell Wood
BFF M1CE

Wait!

The chickens read it with excitement
when it landed on the floor.

Come to my tea
party tomorrow.
See you soon!
Little Mouse
x

"Look!" they said to Cockerel, who raised the party alarm.

Once the sheep and horses knew, it was all over the farm!

Then Sheepdog took the letter and ran over to the wood
to tell as many of his friends about the party as he could.

Fox passed the invite on to Deer, who showed Squirrel in her tree.
Owl woke up from her nap and said, "A party? **Yay! Yippee!**"

She flew over to the dock, where a ship was setting sail.
The letter journeyed through the waves, carried by a friendly whale.

He gave it to a seagull friend
just as she was passing by.

SQUAWK! she went excitedly
and flew into the sky.

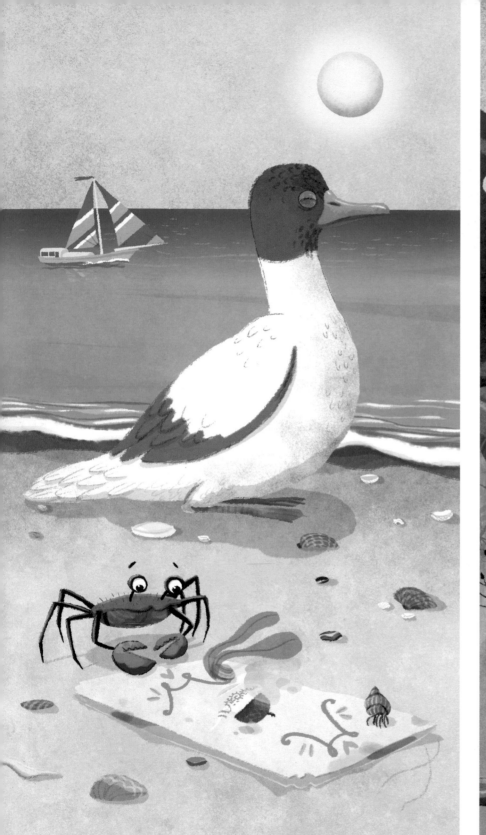

She reached the sandy shore
and dried the invite in the sun.

As soon as she showed
the monkeys they knew
it would be fun!

Their jungle friends joined in and said, "A party sounds just great!
Maybe if we leave right now, we might not be too late."

By the next afternoon, the guests all started to appear.
They'd come from all around the world, each full of happy cheer.

"You must be here for the party!" one called, dancing in the queue.
"I can't wait," replied the next. "It will be so great. **Woo-hoo!**"

Meanwhile, their noisy voices caused the mouse hole walls to shake.

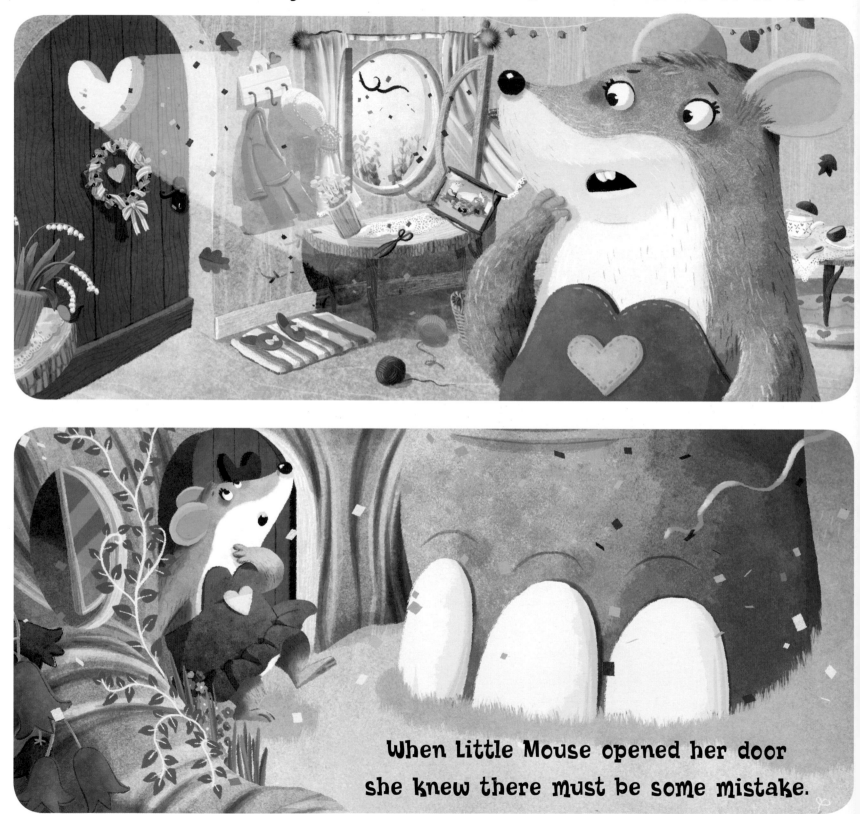

When Little Mouse opened her door
she knew there must be some mistake.

"What are you doing here?" she asked. She couldn't believe her eyes!
"I'm having a small tea party. This is quite a big surprise!"

"We got your invitation," they said. "We thought it was so kind!"
"Well my house is only small," she said. "I hope that you don't mind?"

They all **squashed** and **squished** to fit.

"There's no room!" the animals cried.

"There's only one thing for it," said Little Mouse. "Let's party outside!"

So Little Mouse and her new friends partied long into the night.
They laughed and sang and danced together, till the morning light.

It was the party of a lifetime, complete with the perfect host.
And the whole thing started with a little mix-up in the post.